Howard B. Wigglebottom
Learns About Mud and Rainbows

Written by
Howard Binkow

Illustrated by
Susan F. Cornelison

Written by: Howard Binkow
Illustrated by: Susan F. Cornelison
Book design by: Tobi S. Cunningham

Thunderbolt Publishing
We Do Listen Foundation
www.wedolisten.com

This book is the result of a joint creative effort with Ana Rowe and Susan F. Cornelison.

Gratitude and appreciation are given to all those who reviewed the story prior to publication.
The book became much better by incorporating several of their suggestions.

Rhonda J. Armistead, MS, NCSP, Karen Binkow, Martie Rose Binkow, Leonie Deutsch, Sandra Duckworth, Lillian Freeman, LCSW,
Kim Garretson, Sherry Holland, Renee Keeler, Tracy Mastalski, Teri Poulus, Chris Primm, Laurie Sachs, Anne Shacklett, Mimi C. Savio,
C.J. Shuffler, Nancey Silvers, Gayle Smith, Phyllis Steinberg, Joan Sullivan, Rosemary Underwood and George Sachs Walor.

Teachers, librarians, counselors and students at:

Bossier Parish Schools, Bossier City, Louisiana
Charleston Elementary, Charleston, Arkansas
Glen Alpine Elementary, Morganton, North Carolina
Golden West Elementary, Manteca, California
Iveland Elementary School, St. Louis, Missouri
Lee Elementary, Los Alamitos, California
Meadows Elementary, Manhattan Beach, California
Patterson Primary School, Beaver Falls, Pennsylvania

Payneville Elementary, Payneville, Kentucky
Prestonwood Elementary School, Dallas, Texas
Sherman Oaks Elementary, Sherman Oaks, California
Walt Disney Magnet School, Chicago, Illinois
Westerville City School, Westerville, Ohio
West Navarre Primary, Navarre, Florida
Washington-Franklin Elementary School, Farmington, Missouri

Special thanks to my family for their ideas and support.

Printed in Shenzen, China, by Asia Pacific Offset

First printing: November 2009

LCCN 2009938539

ISBN 978-0-9715390-5-1

This book belongs to

_____

Howard B. Wigglebottom likes to fix things

SO . . . When Mertle couldn't walk fast enough . . .

. . . Howard fixed it.

When the frogs in science class needed to stretch their legs · · ·

. . . Howard fixed it.

10

When Momma complained that
bunny hair was everywhere, even in
the soup . . .

. . . Howard fixed it.

14

When Papa complained he couldn't get to the
paper before the dog did . . .

. . . Howard fixed it.

Yes, Howard was a **BIG** help
to those around him.

So when Howard's best friend was crying at school, naturally he wanted to fix her, too. "What's wrong, Ali? Why are you so sad today?" Howard asked.

Ali explained that her parents have been fighting a lot.
"And it's all my fault!" she sobbed.
Poor Ali, Howard thought. What can I do to fix it?

Each and every day they met.
Ali talked and Howard listened.
But he still couldn't figure out what to do
to help his friend smile again.

Howard decided he needed help.
So he asked the only expert on practically everything in the universe:
his **MOM!**
"I fix things, that is what I do!
But I don't know how to fix Ali and make her feel better," said Howard.

24

"Oh Howard, I'm so sorry Ali is going through such a rough time. Do tell her when parents fight, it's **NEVER** the child's fault! Sometimes parents argue when they have problems. You are doing exactly what Ali needs: you are listening. Sometimes that's what a friend needs most!"

"But I want to **DO** something!" Howard said. "Howard, my dear, no one can fix things all the time. When we find something we can't fix, we can change the way we think and feel about it."

Howard couldn't wait to tell Ali the good news! He was sure it would help her find her smile. Howard looked for her everywhere! Finally, he found Ali in her favorite spot.

"My mom explained everything.
ALI, IT'S NOT YOUR FAULT!" he shouted.
When Howard ran to her, he tripped over his big feet and . . .

. . . fell headfirst into the pond.

When Howard wiped the mud from his eyes, he saw
A WONDERFUL THING!
Ali was laughing just like she used to do.
Then they had the best mud fight ever.
Howard learned that sometimes life gives you **RAINBOWS**
and sometimes you get **MUD**!
So if you find yourself headfirst in mud and you can't change it,
you have choices.

You can be unhappy about it . . .
or make the best of it.

Ali and Howard
were certainly
making the best of it!

Howard B. Wigglebottom Learns about Mud and Rainbows.
Suggestions for Lessons and Reflections

★ IT IS NEVER A CHILD'S FAULT

When Ali learned that the people who take care of her were fighting, she had an awful feeling. What was it? Before they fought, she was happy, joyful and talkative. When they started fighting she felt sad, angry and afraid.

Just like Ali, children think everything bad and ugly that happens around them is their fault. In this book we learn it's never a child's fault when adults fight or separate.

Children don't have the power to stop the rain, make broccoli taste like fries or change the way people feel towards each other. If you believe it's your fault if anything bad happens between grown-ups, think again! It's never a child's fault!

It's OK to feel upset when adults fight. If you would like to feel better or help someone else feel better, try some of the activities at the end of this lesson.

★ FIXING THE THINGS THAT CAN BE FIXED

In this book Howard likes to fix things around the house, be helpful to his friends and make life easier for everyone. It feels good to learn how to fix things and be nice and helpful to others. Here are some ideas for you:

• Find ways to be helpful at home.

• Do a chore someone else usually does before that person has a chance to do it.

• Clean your room before you are asked to do so.

• Help a younger child who is having trouble.

• Ask a grown-up to teach you how to use tools and glue to fix small things.

• Ask an older person if you can help them in any way.

• Look for ways to make things better at school.

When our friends and loved ones feel sad, angry or scared, we can help them a lot just by listening. We don't have to do or say anything special. All we need to ask is, "Please tell me how you feel now" and then listen to the person. Think about the times you felt better just because you told someone you had a problem, a booboo or that your tummy hurt.

★ FIXING THE WAY WE FEEL

Howard was upset when he couldn't fix Ali's problems and make her happy. His mother taught him when we have something or someone we can't fix or make feel better there is one big thing we can do. All of us have the power to change the way we think and feel about people and things. The way to do this is to look for good and positive thoughts.

For example, think of ice cream. A positive thought is to look forward to having ice cream for dessert and remembering how nice it tastes. A negative thought is to get upset because we can't eat ice cream all the time. Everyone likes to be happy. Positive thoughts make us feel good. Negative thoughts make us sad.

In this book, Howard was sad because he thought there was no way to help Ali. When he learned that listening to Ali really was helping her, he felt happy again. All Howard did was to change the way he thought, which made him feel better right away.

When it's raining and we want to go outside and play, we can think about how awful it is because we can't do what we want!

Bet you figured out that's a negative thought. A positive way to think about it is to remember that rain is so important to all the plants and animals. We are so lucky to have a nice roof over our heads and when the rain stops, we can go play outside and look for rainbows! We can find the positive side of almost everything that is happening to us. Sometimes we have to look very hard, but the positive is always there for us to discover.

★ LISTENING TO OUR LOVED ONES

Howard's life became safer, happier and nicer after he learned how to listen to his teachers and parents;* listen to his heart;** and to the little voice in his head.*** In this book Howard learns how to have more fun and feel good when he listens to his friends.

★ ACTIVITIES TO MAKE YOU FEEL HAPPY, HEALTHY AND FRIENDLY

• Read your favorite book.

• Go for a bike ride, a swim or a walk.

• Make a card for someone you like even if it isn't his or her birthday.

• Tell someone you love, "I love you."

• Give someone a compliment. Find something about them you like and tell them about it.

• Make a scrapbook of the foods and things you like.

• Wear your favorite clothes.

• Make a list of all the people you like, in real life and on TV.

• Sing a song you like.

• Dance to your favorite tune.

• Color a picture.

• Play with a pet.

• Call a friend or a relative and ask about their favorite things to do.

• Think of something beautiful and fun.

• Get permission to visit www.wedolisten.com, where you can enjoy free Howard B. Wigglebottom animated books, songs, games, activities, lessons, posters, and E Cards.

Howard B. Wigglebottom Learns to Listen
**Howard B. Wigglebottom Listens to His Heart*
***Howard B. Wigglebottom Learns About Bullies*

31

Learn more about Howard's other adventures.

Books
Howard B. Wigglebottom Learns to Listen
Howard B. Wigglebottom Listens to His Heart
Howard B, Wigglebottom Learns About Bullies

Visit www.wedolisten.com.
Enjoy free Howard B. Wigglebottom animated books, songs, games, activities,
lessons, posters, and E Cards.

You may email the author at howardb@wedolisten.com.

Comments and suggestions are appreciated.